Attack of
The Stacks

By Novid Shaid

Cover art by Rosina Ahmed
rosina.ahmed72@gmail.com

For teachers and students

I

I remember it was lunch time, when I approached the staff toilets, mentally preparing for the next two lessons of the day: Year 7, *A Little Girl Lost and A Little Girl Found*, by William Blake... Nice! And Year 9, *Taming of the Shrew*, studying Katherina's infamous final lines: "your husband is your lord..." Well, they'd really be up for that on a Friday afternoon, wouldn't they! Especially the boys. But then there's always *Shakespeare Retold* on YouTube...

It was the middle of a punishing year of working with supply teachers incessantly needing help with rowdy classes and pressure from above to save the school from an OFSTED assault. Already this year, I had been threatened, sworn at, spat at and bullied. And that was just the staff... Only kidding! I had only been spat at, and that was because a bunch of Year 8s were dribbling spittle down the stairs from the second floor and I happened to walk by.

But it had been a tough year. Trojan horses were

discovered in schools where Muslim teachers taught. Personally, I was impressed because most Muslims I knew were never that organised! The ancient Trojan horse strategy was an awesome display of planning and cunning. Most of the time, us Muslims can't even fill up the shoe racks in the local mosque! But then the media displayed a conveyer belt of schools up and down the country, plotting to overthrow liberal society and transform it into jihad heaven for the men and a pious harem for the women. And it was the Muslim teachers who were to blame...

So, it felt like eyes were on me; my comments were being recorded; my movements studied. Did they know that I used a prayer mat in my classroom that came from Saudi Arabia? With a compass at the top. What would they make of that if they found it? *A prayer compass? God is up in the sky, isn't He? Why do you need a compass for that? Or could this be something else? A tool for secret jihad? A Trojan Horse prayer mat! On the outside, an exotic heirloom, on the inside a navigation system for jihadi takeovers...*

I remonstrated over these things as I sat on the loo, gazing at familiar sights around me: the brand new, toilet furniture of our pristine Academy- may the government be glorified!

As silent as a mouse, I sat (by the way, I tend not to make lots of noise when I'm in the w/c, whilst some of my colleagues like to re-enact fireworks night when they're in the throes of defecation). For a minute, I made a wish that I could make my daily bread in an easier way because, to be honest, teaching English in secondary schools for seventeen years was beginning to take its toll. The constant struggle with marking books, the constant pressure to get good and outstanding lesson observations, the constant fighting and bullying that had to be sorted out. I loved my job and still do. I had always dreamed of being an English teacher.

But now I was beginning to question myself. Could the world of Shakespeare live together with the world of the Quran? Could I continue to be an English teacher, giving my heart and soul to the job and be a pious Muslim at the same time? These questions echoed quietly in my heart ever since those planes struck those towers in Manhattan. Now we were the enemy, and I had been trained to teach English literature and present Western writers. This could spell trouble. The mullahs were becoming over-zealous and power-hungry. Everything Western was evil. And I was a repository of Western literary culture! If ISIS found out, they would hunt me down and force me to erase poetry and prose from my heart and replace them with Jihadi John lectures. And the English were becoming brazenly Islamophobic. Ban the burka; ban the mosques, ban the Muslim English teachers... You can't be both. You can't teach Shakespeare and then go home and tell your wife to wear a burka! Although the closest my wife gets to a burka is a burger: Peri Peri from the local fried chicken place!

Anyway, silence lingered. My mind chattered away. Silence lingered. I readied myself for Year 7. Silence lingered... That's when I first detected that something was up...

2

A hubbub of blistering energetic young voices. That was the typical background muzak mid-way into lunch time. The thumping footsteps of the annoying cretins who rebelled against our ban on using the second floor at lunch time. The screaming of girls hearing about the latest romance. But something had happened outside. You could hear a pin drop. Could it have been an evacuation? Could there have been a fire alarm which I blanked out of my mind because I was so distracted in my Muslim English thoughts? If so, then any minute now, senior staff would be searching the school for me. *Shah is still in the building! There's something fishy going on. He's been teaching ancient Greek myths lately... He's become a Trojan Horse teacher! Seize him!*

Suddenly, I had visions of the principal breaking my cubicle door down and pointing down at me, with the rest of management team peering behind him. I obviously pull up my boxers just in time!

"*Aha! Plotting something in the toilets whilst the rest of us were outside, were we?!*"

And I answer: "*actually, all I was doing was plopping something in the toilet...*"

"*Enough! Call MI5! Arrest him! Ban him! Question him! Water board him! Put him in a room, show him a big hairy rat in a box, then he'll talk!"*

"Or you could use a shrew," I add, *"that would tie in with my Year 9 lessons."*

Then the head teacher advances upon me, grabs me by the scruff of the neck and all the female senior team look away, bar one who says: *"he's wearing Incredible Hulk boxer shorts!"*

The overbearing silence squashed these reveries out of my head and I looked at the Hulk's face staring back at me on my boxer shorts. Yes, I must admit, I was a fan of the big guy! So, I looked at the green man for inspiration on what I should do next.

All I heard back was: "RAAAR!"

This made me pluck up the courage to unlock the door and investigate what was transpiring outside.

I exited the toilet and peered to my right. The corridor which led onwards and forked left and right was deserted. And the stairs to the right which people used to access the first and second floor were also empty. Hmm. Very strange. It must be a fire drill, I thought. Usually the stairs and the corridors were teeming with students coming in and out of the library.

I took an immediate right, facing the corridor which turned left towards my room. Once again empty. Except... In the middle stood a grey chair, perhaps from the adjacent classroom. It was facing the opposite direction. That looked odd, although it could have been one of the kids who left it there for a prank.

I was beginning to feel extremely unsettled. This silence was beginning to spook me out and this random chair in the middle of the hallway seemed ominous. What on earth was going on?

Well, there was only one thing for it. Walk up to the library and peer down into the atrium to see if I could spot anybody. So I was just about to move off when to my horror I noticed the chair in the corridor swivel around, all by itself! As if an invisible hand had turned it. The chair was now facing me. My heart leapt momentarily. The chair stood still while my mind was racing. How did it do that? Was this another prank? Was there invisible string attached to it? The back of my neck shivered for a moment.

I chose to ignore the chair and continued to pace towards the library, where I could stare down into the atrium. And this is what I did. I strode along, like I owned the place, and came up to the barrier and looked below. The vast atrium, filled with tables for children to sit around, was unmistakably empty. I looked forwards and backwards. No children. No staff. Not even any of the cleaners. I walked on to get a better perspective of the whole area. I could now see further into the atrium and the doors beyond. Once again, deserted. The emptiness was eerie. The silence was ominous. Time stood still. It was only then that I made a perplexing discovery. Below, in the atrium, all the tables were exactly where they should be, but all the chairs around them, including the soft comfortable ones that Year 11 love to hog, were gone. Where had all the chairs disappeared to?

This thought was hanging in my head when something caught my attention and I turned to look back at the staff toilets and this is when my day turned surreal.

3

The same chair I had spotted around the corner was now facing me. And what made my heart leap into my mouth was that the chair seemed to be edging its way forward! There was something underhand in the way it slightly tilted at the corner and shuffled forward on its legs that suggested it was following me. I was being stalked by a chair! I had heard of teachers being stalked by psycho pupils, by deranged parents and by other terrifying teachers, but this had to be the first time ever that a teacher was being stalked by a chair!

Then I heard the rumbling of many footsteps flowing up the stairs beyond the chair. Thank God, my hallucinations would finally come to an end as it sounded like the school had finally returned to normality. This must be the kids coming back from the firedrill. But this infernal chair was still edging towards me and I found myself creeping backwards. I heard the double doors crash open to the left behind this miraculous chair. It kept edging towards me. I kept creeping backwards. And then, what I saw left me gaping in horror, confusion, dismay and generally left me scratching my head. For I had realised where all the chairs below had gone to. They had all suddenly burst through the doors and were crowding the corridor behind the first chair like a horde of football hooligans appearing for a rumble. They suddenly stood still. The first chair still crept forwards towards me. The tangled mass behind it seemed to be waiting for something. I was still getting my head around the fact that all the chairs in our school were going loopy, when I heard a high-pitched kind of war cry. Where was it coming from? You wouldn't believe it! It was the first chair! It was emitting a fierce scream. Suddenly all the chairs behind it, the yellow ones and the chunky green ones let out a pounding roar and they all came charging at me!

"AAAH!"

I scarpered like a naughty Year 7 escaping the prefects, thinking to myself: *I am being charged down by a group of screaming chairs. Did someone spike my tea with opium and pork extracts?*

They roared after me like a buffalo stampede, full of wild energy and menace. I sprinted down the corridor, my steps thumping and shuddering along, gasping, terrified, whizzing round to the right, towards my classroom. For a moment, I was clear of them, but I could hear their solid plastic legs thudding along not far behind. I briefly imagined what they would do if they caught up with me. Stab me in the heart with their legs; suffocate me with their cushiony part; bundle on top of me like a gang of rugby players. *Now hang about. What am I saying? Chairs!? Are you out of your mind?* But I had no time to consider this madness because the stampede had reached the corner and I had to surge ahead to stay out of their sight. This I did and, as I was rushing along, I noticed a classroom door ajar: Mr Striker's History class. So, I snuck in, closed the door ever so gently and sat with my back against the door.

A few moments later, I heard the chairs charging past the door in a frenzy. *Phew.* I had a chance to think, but I couldn't pause for too long as they would realise soon I was still on the top floor. I had to think fast.

Before I rationalised what had just taken place, I decided to look around the classroom, and, to my surprise, I saw my colleague, Mr Striker, trapped inside the blinds, rolled up like a long shish kebab in a wrap! Something had torn down the blinds. All the chairs were missing from the classroom and John lay there, wrapped up, with his head and feet sticking out of both ends. He now noticed me:

"Hello Shah!" He was surprisingly upbeat given the circumstances, but he did have an annoying way of addressing me by my surname, even when he passed by me on the way to the bogs. He carried on:

"Well, this is all rather awkward, isn't it?"

I smiled back, "yes, quite awkward." I ducked down and John fell silent because the charging chairs roared past again, which faded away as they continued in their search for me.

"John," I began, "there's something that I have been meaning to ask you."

John stretched his head forward and grinned at me: "okay Shah old chap. Fire away!" It seemed like he was enjoying every minute of his enwrapment!

"What the devil is going on?" I hissed. "Where is everyone? Why are you wrapped up in your blinds? Who did that to you and why? And why in the name of God are the chairs of our school chasing me!"

It felt great to get that off my chest! I sighed momentarily.

"Well Shah. It seems we have been plagued by..."

"Plagued by what?" I pressed him.

"Plagued by..." But he fell silent because we both heard the chairs rush into the room next door, charging around like maniacs.

"You'd better go," John warned.

"But you haven't told me what's going on! What about you?"

"Don't worry. They have me where they want me. You're the only one left Shah, you're the only one left." John motioned me to come closer.

"Listen," he whispered, "you must find the source..."

"Sauce? What do you mean sauce? Tomato sauce? What are you talking about?"

The chairs screamed in anger next door. They seemed to have completed their search of the adjacent room.

"Get out, while you have time! And remember, find the source..." I still looked at him blankly.

"Source with O-U-R Shah." Striker didn't look impressed.

"Oh, I see!" I suddenly felt very stupid.

4

So, John Striker's mysterious request trailed behind me as I gently opened the door and crept away to my left.

I was just about to reach the double doors leading to the stairwell, when I decided to look back. A green cushioned chair, which still had the imprint of a vast backside in it, was looking straight at me. My eyes met its back cushion. Then it shrieked like a psycho and, all of a sudden, the whole gang flooded out of the classroom, rushing towards me. I darted through the doors, flying down the stairs.

Maniacal chairs... Find the source... History teachers wrapped up in giant Venetian blind wraps... I could not fathom for the life of me what on earth was going on. I was beginning to think that my mind was deteriorating, and I was suffering some form of delusion and psychosis. But these misgivings couldn't discount what my very senses were feeling this very second, hearing the pounding legs of these chairs rattling after me as I whizzed down the stairs. One thing was very clear to me now. I had to escape. I had to get the hell out of here. For it appeared that my school had transformed before my very eyes, from a centre of learning and progress, into an incomprehensible mental asylum. And it looked like I could be the only sane person left!

I sprinted downstairs and headed for the doors leading outside. But just as I got halfway down the corridor, a growing mass of chairs rushed into view and blocked the way. There was a great chorus of screams and shrieks. I twisted round and saw that the rest of the horde filled the passage behind me. I was trapped. Stuck in the middle of two gangs of marauding chairs. Both gangs were now slowly and menacingly marching forward in unison and seemed ready to make their final bloodcurdling charge. I only had a split second to decide on my next move. These could be my final moments alive on this earth. I began thinking of what a good Muslim should do when death was approaching. Thinking of my beautiful wife, my lovely children, my loving parents and siblings and... Then the ridiculousness of the situation dawned upon me again and I couldn't help but speak my mind. I patted my chest and cleared my throat.

"Excuse me!" I yelled this at both groups of chairs. They all came to a halt and fell silent, looking at one another in a rather haughty way. *Wait, the human wants to speak to us; we'd better listen to what nonsense he has to say before we punish him for sitting and farting on us since our births.* Well they must have been thinking some kind of chairy thoughts!

"I think there seems to be a misunderstanding here... You are just... chairs!"

Once again, they seemed to be turning to each and saying in chair language: *well you don't say mate!*

I frowned at how silly my previous sentence sounded and carried on:

"This must be a joke. Chairs do not move by themselves and make loud, screeching noises like zombies. You are nothing but a bunch of chairs! Now, whoever is messing around, just put a stop to all this nonsense right here right now!"

The chairs on either side stood still but I could sense that some potent anger was rising in them. Realising my words were ineffectual, I looked around in despair, but then I heard a familiar voice from above me:

"There's no use Abdul. They won't listen."

It was Clive Davies, our principal, staring down at me from the ventilation shaft on the ceiling! He was arching out from an opening wide enough for someone to crawl into.

"Clive?" I remarked dumbfounded, "is that you up there? And by the way it's Abdul Matin not Abdul..." (That always annoyed me.)

Suddenly, the chairs started jumping up and down in unison, a bit like they were stamping their feet. God they were in a bad mood now! The stamping increased in tempo and violence. Thud! Thud! Crash! Crash!

"Ok, sorry, *Abdul Matin*. You'd better get up here because I have a feeling they're going to charge at you any second! Here take my hands!"

Just then the stamping ceased, and chairs rushed at me from all directions, screaming and shrieking. I instinctively jumped up and caught both of Clive's hands and I thank Allah he was a strong bloke! He pulled my arms up and then I managed to take hold of either side of the opening and wrenched myself upwards. The chairs were now directly below, raging, launching at me, but by now I was safely up into this surprisingly wide vent.

"Here, follow me." Clive crawled ahead through the cold metallic shaft. I felt like I was in the middle of a sci-fi horror movie! What if a xenomorph popped its head around the corner... I could hear the chairs beneath us, jumping up and crashing against the shaft. We had to get out of here quickly before they dislodged us from the ceiling.

"Quickly, turn left here, before they smash through the vent," urged Clive.

The shaft forked into two directions: a sharp left and right turn. We took the left and consequently the pandemonium below faded out. The principal crawled ahead, then took another right. I followed and then we found ourselves in a large cavity which was a kind of spaghetti junction for all the different ventilation shafts going around the building. Below was a great grill through which we could see the corridors many metres below.

Our principal, Clive Davies, 'Chunky' as he was affectionately called by the kids because he stood at six foot five and his head was shaped like a cuboid cushion, turned to me and smiled, while he sat perched on the edge of a vent opening.

"So, they didn't get you then."

"Clive, sir, can you explain what the hell is going on. I literally just went to the loos about twenty minutes ago, and, when I emerged, the world had suddenly gone bonkers!"

"Well," began Mr Davies, "after having a good old poo, it can cause a new way of seeing the world."

"What?" I enquired.

"Anyway, anyway... as you can see, Abdul... Abdul Matin, sorry. We are being attacked by some external force."

"Chairs," I added.

"Oh yes, yes, there are the chairs..."

"And I saw John Striker upstairs wrapped up in the roller blinds."

"Yes, our staff have been rather tied up you might say."

"By who or what? What are these chairs? Where

is everybody else?"

"It seems to me, Abdul Matin, that a singular force is controlling these chairs and has made them come alive. We are under attack. The phone lines are down. The external doors are on lockdown and no one knows we're in trouble. I'm sorry to say," now his eyes widened dramatically, "we are on our own..."

"Yes, but how on earth could someone control the chairs in this way? And what about the rest of the school?"

"Well, let me give you a brief picture, Abdul Matin. While you were enjoying your interlude on the loo. There you go, Abdul, internal rhyme... interlude on the loo... thought you would appreciate that as an English teacher... ahem, ahem... yes, where was I? Oh yes, while you were in the loo... And by the way, you must have taken a good twenty minutes in there because I had to let your Year 7s in your classroom."

"Did I?" I was shocked and rather embarrassed.

"Yes, yes, you must have got so carried away that you didn't hear the buzzer."

"Okay, so while I was delayed in the toilets, what happened? Spit it out man!"

"Well, it's kind of hard to explain... one moment everything was normal, the children were as high as kites in the Himalayas after lunch. The next moment, all the chairs just went mental! Dragging pupils and teachers along, thumping, kicking, screeching. They were so strong. Of course, all of us were momentarily in a state of shock. We couldn't understand what was going on. But by the time we could gather our senses, I saw the chairs dragging everyone towards the gym."

"Is that where everyone is now?"

"Yes, that's where they've got the whole school. They're all surrounded by the chairs, in a state of terror!"

"Oh, so how did you manage to get away?"

Clive hesitated and coughed a little, "ahem, ahem... well, I'm one of the few people who knows the ventilation system, so while the chairs were unaware, as it were, I managed to open a vent behind me in a wall and climb up to my escape."

I absorbed what the principal had told me and shuddered at the thought of the whole school community trapped by a horde of hellish chairs.

"Is this really happening? Or is this a nightmare that I'm going to wake from any moment now? I mean, really, who has ever heard of chairs gaining consciousness and terrorising people?"

"Well, it appears they have woken up and are getting everyone back for all their suffering. Chairs have to put up with a lot of stick you know." He almost sounded sympathetic.

"Now come on Clive, seriously! You're not suggesting that some sort of supernatural phenomenon is happening before us, are you?"

"I don't know. But I wouldn't be surprised if someone is behind this, controlling the movements of these plastic terrors."

Suddenly John Striker's comment murmured away in my soul: *find the source... not tomato sauce, source with O-U-R.*

"Okay then, what's the plan?"

"What do you mean?" asked Clive.

"Well, you're the principal, our leader, you must have some kind of plan to get us out of this mess."

"To be honest, I was just going to hang around here until the parents arrived and then one of them would surely call the police..."

"Yes, but what if the chairs attack the parents? What if the chairs get out into the outside world? What if they pass on their disease to all the other chairs out there?"

"Oh, I never really got that far."

"But you're our leader!"

"Yes, I know, but they don't prepare you for supernatural phenomena in head teacher training... I don't suppose you have any ideas do you Abdul? Er... Abdul Matin?" He smiled cheerily.

I slumped against the vent feeling defeated. No

communication; our phones were dead; the doors were guarded. These chairs had somewhat super-human strength and seemed intent on crushing us. It almost felt like the end of the world was nigh... That's when a thought popped into my head. The Prophet, peace be upon him, said, "if the end of the world comes to you and you are planting a seed, continue planting it." This idea reverberated in my mind and heart. I needed inspiration. I thought hard and started praying in Arabic.

"What on earth are you doing?" asked Clive, rather bewildered.

"Oh, sorry, I was just praying."

"Oh, okay, makes sense I suppose..."

I prayed like I had never prayed before. I had never been in this much trouble all my life. Except the episode when a group of grannies and their poodles were chasing us around the local park. Suddenly, a thought arose. I would use the Quran. The Quran would get me out of this mess! Now to most people, it would sound like I was in a state of total desperation by relying on religious texts but bear with me.

"I've got it!"

"You have!? Which is what Abdul?"

"I'll use the Quran to get us out of this mess!"

Clive's enthusiasm suddenly disappeared.

"Your holy book? The Quran? You're not going

to invoke a jihad in this school, are you? Because if you are, then I will have no choice but to let OFSTED know about it."

"No, no. I'm not going to invoke a jihad. No. We can't fight these chairs with our hands and feet. We can't fight them with our minds. This is a supernatural enemy, so we must use supernatural means against them. Beware of the insight of a believer, Clive, for he sees with the light of God..."

"Oh... That's rather dramatic."

"Yes, it is. I am going to use the supernatural power of the Quran, to break through this madness and to find out who or what is behind this and then take them out!"

I think it was the "take them out" part which really impressed Clive: "oh bravo, Abdul, bravo! But how are you going to move around unseen? The little blighters will catch you very quickly."

"That my dear sir is where the Quran comes in..."

Davies looked at me dubiously. I prepared to crawl back into the vent, but before I left, Clive drew me aside.

"Hey, Abdul, you're, er, you're not hiding anything from me, are you? You know, anything along the lines of ancient Greek warfare..."

"No."

"Oh, okay, just asking."

5

It seemed as if my whole life had prepared me for this moment. This moment of truth. It seemed as if there was a reason for me being here, that I did belong in the right place at the right moment. And now my faith would be put to the ultimate test. I was going to turn invisible with the help of the Quran! I was hedging my bets on the famous story of when the Prophet recited certain verses from the Quran to make him invisible from the Meccan elders, who lay outside his home, ready to ambush him. The story went that before he left his house, the Prophet read the verses and walked by the ambushers, completely unseen! My local imam had also claimed that he once recited these verses when he was driving his car whilst his road tax was overdue! A police car suddenly appeared and followed him. He got frightened and began to read the verses. Next thing he knew, the police car carried on as if they had never seen him. Afterwards, we expressed our shock and surprise. Not at the effect of the Quranic verses, but by the fact that he did not have valid road tax. The dodgy mullah!

Anyway, everything was riding on this and I remembered the words of our imam when he related his story.

"You must empty your mind and soul and feel the presence of Allah. Your thoughts must be pure and sacred. Then when you say the verses, you will see the effects!"

Your thoughts must be pure and sacred. Well, as soon as I said this I had flashing images in my mind of luscious strawberry ice cream milkshake, a juicy plate of chicken curry. Right, focus. Pure and sacred thoughts only. I had to do it because, to be frank, I did not have the foggiest idea of how to deal with this situation, never having experienced supernatural phenomena like this before. So, I crept back along the ventilation shaft and held back before the opening. I inched forward and peered down. A group of chairs seemed to be on sentry duty, marching up the down the corridor, anticipating my appearance.

The moment of truth came. It was time for me to read the verses, jump down into the middle of them and walk through invisible, or suffer impalements of chair legs and asphyxiation by cushion cover. I chanted the words in Arabic. I summoned up sacredness and purity in my heart and mind. All I heard back was Clive's voice echoing along the shaft: "are you okay Abdul?"

"Yes, I'm fine, please let me concentrate!"

Focus. Focus. Mind, body, spirit. Let the energy flow.... Suddenly an image of Luke Skywalker appeared before me, followed my Darth Vader and then Princess Leia in that skimpy outfit at the beginning of Return of Jedi. *No, focus on pure sacred thoughts!* Doubts, now, materialised in my head. What if the verses didn't work? What if the chairs attacked me? What if the truth was I was suffering from insanity and when I jumped down I would awaken in a mental hospital?

Sweeping away those clouds of doubts, I found my centre, blocked out everything, I reached out to Allah and recited the verses. Then the real moment of truth arose. My legs hung down from the opening and now I could see two lines of chairs facing each other, seemingly waiting, looking, anticipating. This was my moment. I had to do it. I didn't have a choice. It was do or die. Doubts arose again. When I let go and land on the floor, surely, I would be heard? But I had to take a leap of faith. There was nothing else for it. I closed my eyes and fell downwards, landing with a thump to the floor. The chairs from both sides screamed viciously and charged in my direction. I just sat there, crouching, waiting for my impending doom, my impending death with chair legs sticking out of my head.

Suddenly, I was surrounded by this crowd of angry chairs. They shook, rattled, snarled and leapt violently. I winced, waiting for the first strike. But it never came. In fact, as I glanced upwards, I noticed something strange about their behaviour. They seemed to have paused and were looking all around the corridor and there I was sitting in the middle of them! They went perfectly still, only a few metres away from me, scanning the area and I sat, with the exhilaration flooding through me because I realised something- it worked! The verses had made me invisible!

To prove this to myself, I did something risky. I stood up straight, towering over the chairs, and, to my delight, they continued looking in the opposite direction. Every now and then, one of them came close to me and I backed off slightly to avoid contact. Moments passed. They could not find me, so they started moving off, seemingly troubled by the noise they had heard and puzzled by the origin. In a few minutes, they marched away and began searching for me elsewhere in the building.

6

I marvelled at this miracle and went up to a classroom window to see my reflection. Amazing! The wall opposite reflected at me. I was a spirit! I was the invisible man! H G Wells would be proud of me! Momentarily, I remembered that my road tax was running out soon. This could come in handy.

Now I knew I had to check out the main hall for myself. I had to discover what had happened to the rest of the school. So, I crept along the hallway and stopped before the passage turned right. I peered ahead. The chairs had just reached the double doors and rushed up the nearest stairwell, probably looking for me. Excellent! The coast was clear. Even though I was now invisible, I wasn't taking any chances, knowing that I couldn't keep my thoughts pure and sacred for a long time. I was not going to reach a sanctified spiritual station any time soon, with my penchants for science fiction, strawberry milkshake and wild nights of five-a-side football. Therefore, I moved forward, carefully, nervously, not knowing when and where the invisibility would wear off. The impression I got from the story of the Prophet, peace be upon him, was that he was invisible for a short space of time. I had to hurry.

The growling and screeching of the chairs disappeared up the stairs just as I came through the double doors. I glanced to the right into the vast atrium. Nothing. So, with confidence, I began to move left towards the hall when I came face to face with a repulsive chair. Yuck! It was from the PE office with bulging cushions, spindly legs with its metallic frame glinting in the light. It was looking straight at me... I held my breath. It stood perfectly still, looking straight into me. Then it rambled off through the double doors. Phew! That was a close one. For a minute, I thought the miracle had worn off.

I progressed through the next set of double doors, past the admin offices to the right. The computer screens were paused on their respective screen savers: Idris Elba in a heroic pose, the Himalayas and one showing a happy family sitting together. I looked closer at the picture. It was Jessica, our exams officer. She was sitting proudly with her husband and kids, reposing on these ornate, antique chairs in some stately home. Probably a wedding shot by the looks of their apparel. I frowned as I noticed how beautiful and still these majestic chairs looked with their arabesque patterns etched in gold on the arm rests and lavish back rest. These chairs adorned their houses and provided comfort to the people, but our chairs had woken up and were terrorising us. If this is how chairs felt, then imagine if everything else woke up. Imagine the nightmare that bins and trash cans would give us if they became conscious? My appreciation for inanimate objects suddenly changed. From this day on, I would never see things in the same light...

Right, I was here, standing before the hall. The glass in the doors was obscured so I would have to open the doors. This was a risky move. There might be a chair right next to the door, but the curiosity was too much. So, I gently nudged the door forward. Nothing stopped its progress, so I pushed it some more to create enough space to slip through.

I did this and now looked around me. The sight left me speechless. The hall was a vast auditorium with staging at the far end and the flags from various countries hanging down from lines of spotlights and fixtures on the ceiling. But it was the floor area which took my breath away. There was a vast circle of chairs, of all shapes and sizes, facing inwards, growling, gnashing. In the middle of this circle, I could see the whole school population, sitting down on their buttocks, holding their knees together, cowering. Everyone was there, the teachers, staff, cleaners, pupils, even some visitors. Whenever someone looked up, a chair came up and clobbered them on the head, leaving them wincing. It was horrible. Like a group of the gestapo had herded the school together, preparing them for execution.

At the edge of the group, I could make out the Year 9 brat, Mickey Sykes, whose chief aim was to get teachers sacked. He looked up momentarily in fright, and suddenly a bottle-blue chair gave him an almighty smack on the head. I couldn't help it... A burst of laughter erupted from me and then subsided quickly. Just the sight of that little devil receiving a smack sent joy into my veins, but this was short-lived because the real terror in Mickey's face made me feel instantly guilty. And, also, there was the slight problem of every single chair staring in my direction! I kept exceptionally still. Once again, I did not know if the invisibility had worn off. I guess I would find out in these very moments...

Every chair looked towards me, although the people seated daren't raise their heads. These chairs had sent the frights, even into the likes of Mr Murray, our six-foot PE teacher who specialised in rugby and knocking people out on a Friday night, the beast! At this moment, monster Murray, as the kids liked to call him, sat, cowering in the middle of the huddling masses. He was known to be superstitious and always found a way to take Fridays off when they fell on the 13th. The sight of someone like him in a state of fear did nothing to solidify my resolution.

Anyway, before the chairs could act, I edged backwards, while the chairs still locked their gazes towards me. The door must have been inches from me now. My plan was to slip quietly through the door and to make the least amount of noise on Earth.

Then a loud creak echoed through the hall. My bottom had pushed too early against the blasted door, which was evidently very squeaky. (I made my mind up there and then that if I made it out of this alive, I was going to give our wily, cannabis-chewing caretaker, Mr Reynolds, a piece of my mind!) This negative impulse to Mr Reynolds shot through me and now I looked ahead. The chairs were focussed straight at me and launched themselves; evidently the invisibility had worn off.

"Oh crap!" I shouted. The chairs charged towards me. My inner backbiting and swearing must have broken the blessings of the Quranic verses that rendered me invisible. I would have to find somewhere to sincerely repent to Allah and recite the verses again, but I had no time now as I flew through the doors, followed by a line of bloodthirsty classroom chairs, screaming behind me. I sprinted back towards the atrium, through the double doors. But then a crowd of chairs was waiting for me in front of the Atrium, growling with delight, shooting straight at me.

I took an immediate right and flew up the stairs, heading for the second floor. They were gaining on me fast! What was I going to do?

I reached the second floor and rushed past the toilets, that place where it all started, and then sprinted towards the library, hoping that the chairs didn't appear from the other end. I was just passing the library doors, when I noticed a figure sitting, with hands covering the face. The chairs had reached the doors and were charging towards me. But I still looked at this person, trying to figure out who it was. It was a girl. I knew her... She looked very familiar. I could see that although she was covering her face, she was looking through her fingers, straight at me. Grace Morgan... The sad, little Year 7 girl, who suffered terrible bullying at the hands of some nasty Year 9 girls. Grace Morgan... I had to save her! She was probably petrified, in a state of shock and if the chairs found her, who knows what they may do. But I could not pause any longer because the marauders behind me were gaining fast, so I whipped around the corner. Suddenly, I saw a hand beckoning me from a classroom door ahead on the right. Who on earth could that be? So, without a moment's hesitation, I rushed towards the door and grabbed hold of the hand, which, to my surprise, yanked me in with tremendous power...

7

The door shut in a flash and I found myself being bear-hugged by some female whom I could not recognize. Oh dear. We had to inch away from the door because the demon chairs charged by in a frenzy, pounding down the corridors and down the stairs in search of me. Phew! Then I observed the current dilemma I was in. A healthy female was currently squeezing me so hard that I thought my ribs would crack and I feared that my wife would walk in at any moment and smack me on the head with her rolling pin for fooling around with mysterious women.

"Okay, could you let go of me, please?" I gasped.

"Have they gone? Have they gone?" She whispered frantically.

Hmm, that voice sounded familiar. It could be one of three people... Then the penny dropped.... *Oh, shucks...* It was the deputy-head, Floella Smith, the immensely strong and healthy PE teacher, who could beat everyone in an arm-wrestling match, even Monster Murray. But, for some reason, Floella always acted rather coy and embarrassed with one or two male members of staff, me included. I probably reminded her of her dad, I hoped. I couldn't bare to contemplate any other reason I brought these reactions in her. These thoughts aside, I managed to emit some sounds of distress.

"Floella.... It's me... Abdul Matin ... you can let go now... they've gone..."

She suddenly relaxed for a moment and registered what I had said and who she had enveloped in her powerful embrace.

"Oh Abdul!" And then she gave me a stronger, almighty hug and I felt like I was being crushed. "Oh Abdul... Thank God... I've been every so afraid!"

I thought for a moment- you don't need to be afraid of anything love!

"Okay..." I managed. "Don't worry... Could you just let me go for a bit?"

And praise be to Allah, she finally let go! I felt my bones settling and my ribs sighing in relief. To my horror, I noticed that Floella was slightly blushing and fanning her face. "Oh, thanks Abdul," she smiled, "I knew someone would save us." She fanned her face again and smiled at me.

Oh crap, I better dispel this atmosphere very quickly.

"Floella," I began.

"Just call me Flo, Abdul, that will help me to relax."

The atmosphere remained cloudy; I tried to steady my thoughts through contemplation.... No, all that came to mind was Wonder woman, 1984.

"Okay, right, Flo, let's be really focussed here, can you tell me how on earth you got here and if you've managed to contact the police?"

"Well, where should I start?" she remarked, as if recalling an incident with a class from hell: "First, we were all screaming because the chairs went doolally; then it was just pandemonium with people running for their lives and the chairs bounding after them, so I managed to snuck up into this room and wait until further orders..." She smiled, rather guiltily.

"And the police?"

"I tried my phone, but for some reason I'm not getting any signal..." She said, looking at her phone again and checking.

"Hmm... There is something amiss in all this nonsense; something that is just really bugging me... But forget that, we need to think of something... Erm, Floella?"

"Yes?" she asked innocently

"Could you let me past please?" She was now blocking my way, staring straight into my eyes, preventing me from walking past and thinking.

"Oh, sorry, honest mistake."

"We have to do something..."

"Yes, how about you stay here with me in this room, and we can just wait here together, while the world goes crazy outside; watch the setting sun of humanity sink into the oblivion ..." Her voice was softening, and she had now stuck her nose onto my right shoulder.

"No," trying to nudge her back without success, "we have to do our duty... We have to save this school!"

Floella suddenly dislodged her nose from my shoulder, took a long deep satisfied sigh and pushed me against a nearby table, leaving me sprawling.

"Right, Shah, enough of this fooling around. You have served your purpose as a piece of eye candy to settle my nerves, now, as deputy head of this asylum, I am going to take the bull by the horns, show them who's boss, and put these chairs back where they belong!"

"And where is that?" I asked, rather meekly.

"Right underneath my buttocks!"

And with that, Floella suddenly brandished a large baseball bat from behind the desk and stood ready at the door.

"Are you going out there? To face them?"

Floella's eyes flashed, baring her teeth like David Banner transforming into the hulk. "Of course! Are you gonna join me, or are you just gonna stand there like a poodle waiting for mummy?!" Floella certainly meant business and seemed like she was in an awesome mood, so I joined her on the other side of the door. She passed another baseball bat to me and smiled wickedly.

"I managed to pick these up whilst I got away. You ready."

"Ready when you are Flo."

She smiled: "you look cute when you're all riled up."

I didn't quite understand what the plan was apart from swinging and bashing as many chairs as we could, which sounded rather satisfying but I feared they could still overpower us.

"1, 2, 3," she whispered, "let's break some chairs!"

We flew outside.

8

After wrenching open the door and standing in *bash them up* stance, we both found ourselves surrounded by the horde, seething, sneering, shaking their legs, rattling their backs.

Floella looked into my eyes like a Germanic barbarian and screamed: "Fight!!!"

And then all hell broke loose. Floella launched into the nearest chairs, like Boudica facing off the Romans. She swung wildly, battering, thumping, pummelling, whilst roaring like a lion. The chairs flew black violently against the walls, splayed about on their backs, wriggling their legs like capsized woodlouse. I followed suit, screaming: "ALLAHU AKBAR!" Suddenly Clive Davies's face appeared above, outside the air vent, looking at me disapprovingly: "I will definitely call PREVENT after all this Shah... Ahem, ahem... Anyhow, carry on! Tallyho!"

I ignored Clive and plunged right into the thick of

it, swinging the baseball bat as if it was a Saracen sword, watching, satisfyingly, as the chairs fell against the walls.

"That's the spirit Shah!" Yelled Floella, smacking a jumping chair right in the cob, "show them you're not just a pretty face with sumptuously long eyelashes!"

I was now desperate to look at a mirror... Sumptuously long eyelashes!

Anyway, we seemed to be making an impression on the horde, as they were now retreating from both sides.

Floella came charging at me and gave me a whopping high five.

"Wooohhee!" She was loving this. I was now holding my aching left hand, trying not to cry. Then there was momentary silence. The sprawling chairs had all gotten up, brushed themselves down and lingered off in either direction, seemingly wary of our baseball bats and attacking prowess. The swinging doors from both sides suddenly burst open, and the chairs moved apart to let something through. Floella tightened her grip around her baseball bat. I gulped. Perhaps it was time to read those invisibility verses again. But I was unable to focus my mind and heart. For what stood on both sides of the corridors were two humungous green cushioned chairs, like champion wrestlers, facing us down.

"Oh dear…" I managed to say.

"Oh yes… I like it… Come to mamma!" replied Floella.

It was obvious what was going on here. They wanted to challenge us one to one. A bit like the duels before the commencement of a pitched battle. For me this was a David versus Goliath situation. For Floella, this was a ruckus every Friday night at the rugby club!

"So, you want some do yer!" Floella growled. The chair on her side seemed to sneer and snarl in response. "Okay then, let's do this!" And she charged towards the giant chair, with her baseball bat raised. The chair stormed at her likewise like a raging bull. I watched in astonishment, in amazement, but also in horror at the thought of us surviving this and encountering Floella in the car park after school… Back to the charge, Floella brought the baseball bat thundering down on the beefcake chair. It ricocheted and somersaulted from the impact, and then fell to the ground, facing the other way. Floella looked back at me with a triumphant smile. But in that moment, the chair suddenly twirled around and walloped Floella in the midriff momentarily winding her so that she now sat against the wall like an ailing granny, raising her hand for assistance. Uh-oh… Now the big bully chairs brought their attention to me and started charging at full speed. And through plain instinct and fluke, I managed to jump aside just before impact and the two hulks smashed against each other and kind of knocked themselves out!

"Good going Shah!" coughed Floella, getting her breath back. The two monster chairs were shifting slightly and twitching their legs. They were coming to their senses... The horde on either side rumbled and rattled, ready for another attack. Floella seemed to have lost her gusto and said: "Shah, I think it's time to run. You go left I'll go right." But before I could reply, she shot out of the main door to the right and scampered down the stairs. Then the chairs from both sides bounded towards me. There was nothing for it. I ran up to one of the monster chairs, which still looked drowsy, heaved it up, swung it round and round and hurled it to the coming chairs, knocking a whole row off their legs like skittles. In that moment of confusion I raced through the fallen chairs back towards the library and main stairs, with the horde charging behind me. I kept running until I remembered the girl. Grace Morgan in Year 7. And there she was again, still sitting there, probably in shock, covering her eyes, sitting against the library doors. The chairs had still not noticed her. I didn't want the chairs to approach her direction, so instead of taking the main stairs by the library, I took the nearest exit door and stairs. The chairs came roaring not far behind me, including the green monsters who, from their rattling, seemed furious. Floella was nowhere to be seen. I carried on leaping down the stairs, heading for the ground floor, creating some distance between them. I jumped down the last flight of stairs and landed awkwardly and fell to the ground. Thank God none of the kids saw that and recorded. I would've become a Youtube or Tiktok star overnight for the wrong reasons. But then, in between the stairs, I saw two pairs of eyes, which seemed to be giggling.

"Mr Shah!" That was Trudy King's voice.

"What are you doing on the floor?" That was Jayden Clark's voice. Two of my least favourite students in the school. Trudy was prone to slurping on energy drinks, asking for loos breaks every lesson, and giving constructive comments on my dress sense. Once, during an Ofsted inspection Trudy told the inspector that he was wearing the same suit as me. Cheers for that Trudy. Jayden Clark is every teacher's nightmare. Every two minutes he makes ridiculous comments. Just imagine it, we're reading the last part of Of Mice and Men, and every paragraph Jayden pipes up with: "Is he going to kill him sir? Is this where he shoots him? I bet you he's gonna shank him in the back..."

Reluctantly, I joined the two bozos under the stairs.

"Hi Mr Shah." said Trudy. I hesitated, looking

down at my shirt and tie.

Jayden followed suit: "right on Mr Shah! Right on!" Oh, shut up Jayden.

But then we went silent and hid further under the stairs, as the chairs came roaring down and burst through the doors. When the coast was clear, I looked at the two kids crouching with me and thought about what on earth I was going to do next. Then Jayden looked at me and opened his mouth: "Is it legal for you to hide under the stairs with us?"

9

Jayden, Trudy and I stalked the corridors, like a trio of wannabe ninjas on a mission. Doors were shut, and the classrooms were all deserted as if it were the school holidays. It also seemed like the chairs were on holiday as every room we passed had been emptied of them. But we could hear them on the floors above, rattling and thudding along like torrential rain banging on a tin roof, searching the school for us renegade humans. I touched a door as I walked past. Yes, I was awake; this was real; and above, preternatural chairs were on the rampage. This day had certainly turned out to be an eventful one; one to tell the grandchildren about whilst reposing on an armchair that would hopefully not tear you to pieces!

"Right you lot." I whispered, bringing us to a halt. "We need to discuss our next steps."

"Next steps?" asked Jayden, blankly.

"Yes, our next steps, our plan, our main objectives." God this was going to be hard work.

"What, like the three-part lesson objectives that Miss Right writes on the board?" Trudy suddenly went into one: "All of us should be able to escape; most of us should be able to escape without getting killed; and some of us should be able to escape without losing a limb. Like that?" She twinkled her eyes at some imaginary boy she fancied.

"No." Inwardly I was horrified at this girl's rationality levels. "I mean the steps we need to take to save ourselves and the school."

"Steps," commented Jayden. "Well I think there are certainly some steps we could take to get out of here."

Hmm, he might be onto something. "Okay, what do you have in mind?" I asked.

"Well, we could take the steps from the playground that go down to the side gates, then we'd be home and free." replied Jayden, innocently.

I despaired for the future of British children for a few seconds and then replied: "No, we don't need lesson objectives, or steps leading up or down to heaven. What we need is very straightforward. A plan to get out of here."

"Yes," replied Trudy. "My English teacher always says you should have a plan before you write your story."

"Yes," added Jayden. "And my DT teacher always says you should fill out planning sheets before embarking on design work. So I agree with the planning."

"Ooookay," I rolled my eyes and sighed. "So I think-"

"Sir, are you okay?" enquired Trudy.

"Sure, I'm fine, as I was saying-"

"It looked like there was something wrong with your eyes," added Jayden.

"No, my eyes are fine, I was just-"

"Don't worry sir, I know this must be very stressful for you, but I'm sure we will find a solution to this problem."

"Thank you Jayden, thank you, but I'm not really that stressed, and my eyes are just fine, I was only-"

"You don't have to make excuses for us sir," continued Trudy, as if she was the school councillor. "Just let it all out; let it all flow; say everything you want to say or just be silent and allow your subconscious to naturally emerge and flow out without any inhibitions, without any obstacles, without any fear..." For a minute, I could swear she was trying to put on a Joanna Lumley voice.

"That's quite a speech and therapy session Trudy," I said.

"Yes sir, Trudy is a natural."

"Agreed Jayden, I can see Trudy going into counselling in the future. But shouldn't we get back to our plan?"

"Cheers!" exclaimed Trudy.

"No, not at all, I think you just gave a great speech there Trudy, well done!"

"Cheers!" she exclaimed again, looking in the opposite direction.

"As I said, no need to thank me..."

"No sir, CHAIRS!" Suddenly Trudy and Jayden ran in the opposite direction, and before me a horde of chairs came thundering towards us.

"Run!" I screamed and bolted after the two students.

Behind, all we could hear was high-pitched screaming, rattling legs, and frenzied movements. The two were just ahead now and we had made some gains on the chairs. We burst through a set of doors, a few seconds ahead and raced around the corner. The chairs weren't far behind. Just then, we saw an arm and hand beckoning us from the storeroom door next to the science labs.

"There quickly!" We scarpered towards the extended arm and disappeared into the darkness of the storeroom...

10

A few seconds later, in the darkness, I could feel heavy breathing and my ribs being squeezed by an almighty force.

"Thank God I found you Shah…"

It was Floella bearhugging me again.

"Flo.. el.. la-" I gasped. "Please let me go-"

"Is that you miss?" asked Trudy, pleasantly surprised.

Suddenly Floella relaxed her grip and I breathed for my life. "Yes, but we must whisper…. Is that you Trudy?"

"Yes Miss Smith. Good to hear your voice!"

"And I'm here too, Jayden." whispered Jayden in the darkness.

"Ah wonderful! At least we have two brave and intelligent children as part of our freedom squad."

Intelligent… I despaired inwardly. Brave. Well, I couldn't disagree with that; both had run like coyotes from the chairs, but: "Hang about.. What do you mean by freedom squad?"

The chairs streamed past outside, howling and braying. "Freedom squad Shah," Floella continued in the darkness. "We are going to take these chairs head on and kick them back into the dark ages…"

"Great fighting talk Floella, but we need more of a plan then kick them back to the dark ages…"

A rather eerie vibe seemed to permeate the air.

"Hang on..." I said. "Something is not right... Speaking of darkness, what is this room?"

"This is the science storeroom." answered Jayden.

"How do you know so much about it?" whispered Trudy.

"Well, because I always skive in here when we got a supply teacher for Science." sniggered Jayden "And it's nice and comfortable in here..."

"How is that?" The eeriness was palpable for me, but I couldn't think why.

"Oh, coz there's always plenty of chairs in here," remarked Jayden casually.

"Chairs?" uttered Floella.

"Yeah, stacks of em..." The penny dropped and he went silent. We heard a slight shuffling behind us in the darkness.

"Use your phone," muttered Floella to me.
I took my phone out my pocket, ever so gently, and switched it on. The dim screen appeared but there was no phone signal. I selected the torch app and shone it behind momentarily.

To our horror, we noticed five, large stacks of chairs facing the other way. In the gloom, I decreased the torch light intensity, my hand beginning to tremble. We all looked behind and then at each other putting fingers to our lips and pointing towards the door. We had to get out of here as quickly and as quietly as possible without alerting these chairs. God knows how they had not noticed us earlier. Perhaps they were not infected like the other chairs in the school because they were so hidden away. Anyways, we all edged towards the door, feeling our way on the floor, making the least noise as possible. What would happen if they sensed us? Would we be trapped in here and attacked? My pulse was going haywire and I could tell the two kids, previously quite blasé about the situation, were now shuddering in fear. I shone the weaker, blue light towards the chairs again. All still. All facing the other way. No reaction. Good. We continued shuffling along, praying that the marauding chairs outside were far off. Now we were by the door. Light crept in through the gaps and we could see each other's faces. I signalled Floella to take hold of the handle, whilst we all stood up behind her ready to get out of there.

"After three," I whispered. "Open it." Floella nodded took a hold of a handle, whilst I counted down with my fingers. I got to three. She took hold of the handle and turned it. Suddenly, we heard a great swish in the storeroom. I shone the torchlight at the chairs. We froze momentarily. The stacks had now all turned around and seen us. They were awake! And ready to attack!

"Run!" I yelped. And then a chorus of screaming

filled the air as the chairs disentangled from the stacks and came after us and we burst through the doors.

Just as we came back into the light of the corridor, the chairs in the storeroom burst out, and more came rumbling from the other corridor, so we bounded towards the first-floor doors, ascending the steps. The chairs were gaining on us. We got to the next floor and made a run for it. I noticed the storeroom for the languages department and guided the three of them in.

"Here you lot, get in here, while I make a distraction."

Floella turned to me; her eyes melting: "Shah, be careful..." And she was just about to plant a kiss on my cheek when I pushed them into the room. Phew! Then the chairs burst through onto the first floor.

"Oi! You horrible lot, come and get me!" They charged at me, and I screamed for my life, sprinting down the Languages corridor with the cretins on my heals. I took the stairs to the next floor, sending the chairs tumbling over each other, which gave me a few seconds to spare. Now on the second floor, I found myself in a familiar place- the English corridor. Directly opposite I could see the library across the atrium. Amazingly, Grace Morgan was still there seated by the door, covering her eyes. My goodness me, someone had to get her out of there!

But thoughts aside, the stacks were hot on my heals and I had to hide somewhere to gather my thoughts. So, I disappeared into the door behind me, my colleague, Mrs Pearson's room and hid for a while until the coast was clear. The doors crashed open outside, and hid further in the room, waiting for the flood of chairs to come roaring past. They did. I was safe for a while. It was then that on the table next to me I noticed a blue, English exercise book. On the bottom line said, Mrs Pearson. The line above it. Year 7 English. Then my eyes widened and my mouth formed an O. The top line said, Grace Morgan....

II

Grace Morgan's exercise book... Something was telling me to open it and have a good read.

I looked through the exercise book to find the most exquisite English work and writing. Beautifully presented, underlined titles, meticulous work. Grace was a wonderful student. However, I noticed that the pages at the back were outlined in colour. So, I went to the back. That was when the eerie feeling returned and started to grab a hold of me, squeezing the life out of me. Actually, I was just having a flashback of Floella, which made me tremble. Anyway, the creepiness was certainly in the air, as the back of the book was a complete contrast to the front. Grace had coloured the back page in red, and then in black had written the following, troubling lines in a demented handwriting style:

They all hate me... They all despise me... I am truly lost like Lyca... And they are all beasts...

This didn't seem to be the writing style of a Year 7 student. This was a more thoughtful and bitter mind. The next page was still troubling. She had once again decorated the page in demonic dark red shades and this time, she had written some verse from William Blake that we were studying with year 7 from Little Girl Lost:

'Lost in desert wild
Is your little child.
How can Lyca sleep
If her mother weep?

Sleeping Lyca lay,
While the beasts of prey,
Come from caverns deep,
Viewed the maid asleep.

My eyes were rivetted on her writing below the poem. *These will be my opening incantations.* Incantations for what? My heart felt sick. Striker's words appeared before me, *look for the source...*

Then, on the next page, I found a page ripped from another book, ancient, parchment-style. At the top was the book's title: *A Handbook For Witchery.* I took a deep gulp. Then what I read on this ripped page had me frozen on the spot. The subheading for this page was: *Bewitching Objects For Vengeance*

And it read: *First you need to decide, dear friend, on an opening incantation, then focus your internal energy on an object of your choice. Once you have achieved this, pour your thoughts, intentions and vengeful feelings into the object, and even summon every object of the same kind, and let them all do you bidding... But be aware, you will need to choose your own closing incantation to stop the bewitchery.*

My eyes were glued to this very page and then what lay beneath it in jagged writing, Grace's handwriting. *I will make them all pay! I will make them feel the fear! I will bring their destruction from where they least realise it!*

Then underneath, she had begun to write the closing incantation, but I couldn't make out the letters.

Witchery... Grace Morgan... Vengeance... I brooded over the fact that Grace was certainly a sad, bullied girl in year 7 who had hardly any friends. I mourned at the fact that she was a lost soul, who probably only wanted some kind company and a chat. And I trembled at the potential reality, that Grace Morgan, that sweet little girl in the year 7, had invoked the wrath of God, or some evil spell upon the whole school, and judgement would soon come down upon us.

I walked out of the door; the chairs nowhere in

sight, and walked up to the barrier, which faced the library door on the other side of this floor, with the wide atrium space in the middle. Grace Morgan had sensed me and now stood up and looked me straight in the eye- her eyes were clouded and filmed over as if in a trance. Then she shrieked with great power: "My beasts! Feast on him!" Chairs came from both sides charging at me. They were Grace Morgan's beasts!

There was only one way out of this. I had to get to Grace and break her from her trance and end this spell of vengeance which she had invoked upon the school. Real life had now turned into a supernatural thriller! I would have to exorcise her; pull the evil spirits from her soul and from the plethora of chairs in our school. Well, I felt well-armed for this moment as I could use the Quranic verses from earlier on. In fact, I tried to read the invisibility verses again, but I couldn't focus as I had too many visions of chairs and Floella tumbling towards me.

Anyway, I had a split-second plan that I had gleaned from action-thriller movies. The beasts as Grace called them were now coming at me from each side: blue, green, computer chairs with their back swivelling around like a grinder. Just before they touched me, I leapt onto the barrier and then held on for dear life, while hundreds of chairs leapt into the air and fell metres and metres below onto the ground floor atrium area in a great crash! The legs dangled dangerously in the air, and suddenly Clive stuck his head of out a shaft above me: "Tally ho Shah! Great work!" And quickly disappeared into the shaft.

"Thanks..." I grimaced and wrenched myself back up, saving myself from a crippling drop to the ground floor.

With no chairs in sight I rushed towards Grace, who was seated again on the floor, covering her eyes with her hands, seated against the library door.

I approached her, gently.

"Grace, it's me. Mr Shah. Are you okay?"

No response. She sat motionless; her hands covering her eyes. An evil presence flowed around her and crowded around me. I immediately read the invisibility verses from the Quran and others which settled my soul. However, Grace, in an exceptionally creepy way, looked at me through her fingers, making a gap, and laughed under her breath, an evil laugh.

"You will have to do better than that..." She sniggered; her eyes clouded menacingly. Then she screamed: "My beasts! Come to me!"

I peered at the squirming chairs below. They had all regrouped and rushed for the stairs in a great gang. What was I going to do now?

"Please, Grace, please, stop this, before someone gets really hurt."

Grace now dropped her hands and spoke. "Before someone gets really *hurt*? *Hurt*? Do you know how it feels to be really hurt by the community around you? To be cast out like a lost soul.... Like Lyca. Lost with the beasts? Well, I have awoken my beasts, and now I will make everyone feel the hurt that they have made me feel, sir."

This wasn't working. She was too bitter and hurt. I had to try something else. But what? Any minute now the chairs would be upon me. The beasts would finish me off. The book! The exercise book! That was it. Suddenly, a saying of the Prophet, peace be upon came to my mind: "Received wisdom is the lost-she camel of the Muslim." In this case, wisdom was William Blake and his poem Little Girl Lost, which Grace seemed to be enamoured by. She had even used some verses from the poem as an opening incantation.

I started to chant the verses, passionately:

'Lost in desert wild
Is your little child.
How can Lyca sleep
If her mother weep?

Sleeping Lyca lay,
While the beasts of prey,
Come from caverns deep,
Viewed the maid asleep.

They were having no effect. I had to work out the closing incantation! It must be from the complementary poem: "Little Girl Found". But I could hardly remember the verses. The screaming of the horde was getting closer. I wracked my brains for the lines. Grace Morgan just sat there smiling, watching the world turn into flames around her. I suddenly remembered the last verses of the poem:

'Follow me,' he said;
'Weep not for the maid;
In my palace deep,
Lyca lies asleep.'

As I invoked these verses, the chairs smashed through the second-floor doors and came tumbling onto the floor. Grace seemed to shift in her space and started mumbling under her breath. I continued:

Then they followed
Where the vision led,
And saw their sleeping child
Among tigers wild.

Now the chairs turned to my direction and advanced menacingly. Grace was now writhing as she sat, screaming out, as if possessed. The chairs launched at me with their legs aimed at my head. I was at the end of my tether with fear and felt as if my life was now over, before I exclaimed:

To this day they dwell
In a lonely dell,
Nor fear the wolvish howl
Nor the lion's growl...

And then all the chairs fell in a lifeless heap on the floor before me; Grace fell to the ground as if asleep, and I shouted out a praise to the Lord,

"Alhamdulillah!"

Grace came to her senses, as if she had been in a long sleep. Her kind eyes shone out and she spoke with confusion: "Mr Shah? What happened?" She looked at me and chairs scattered around us. "Why am I here?" I looked at her, slightly hesitant, but glad she was speaking normally.

"Don't worry Grace. It's all going to be okay now. You are safe with me..."

And with that I led her back through the trails of lifeless chairs. So strange it was to see them lying there still, on the floor, on the stairs, entangled in a complete mess.

By the time we reached the ground floor, we heard a rumble of voices and the whole school came pouring through into the atrium. Our head teacher Clive Davies appeared, as did Floella, Mr Striker, Trudy, Jayden and all the students and teachers crowded around us.

"Well done Shah!" exclaimed Striker. "You found the source then!"

"Well done Shah," smiled Floella, coyly. "You stood your ground. Perhaps you could join our staff rugby club..."

"Shah, my friend." exclaimed the headteacher. "Well done! Well done old chap! Whatever you did, you managed to repel the attack of the stacks! Hopefully we will be safe from these critters and can use them to plant our bottoms on! How did you manage it?"

I looked down at Grace, who seemed to have remembered the whole event, and was looking very embarrassed. "Oh, I just prayed for success, and it seemed to work." Grace looked at me from the corner of her eyes and smiled with appreciation.

"Well," began Clive, addressing the whole school, "I think we all need to have an enjoyable afternoon, seeing as we've all been so overexcited and assaulted by these hallucinations of zombie chairs and objects moving by themselves. A bunch of hocus pocus if you ask me. Ahem, ahem. Anyway, anyway. I announce that from now until hometime, we will have an extended break!"

The whole school came alive with cheers from the teachers and students. Students and staff walked gingerly around the fallen chairs and streamed outside into the playground; the relief clear on their faces.

The headteacher's PA, Mrs Worthy approached us. "Mr Davies, I have checked the CCTV, and unfortunately, it was all malfunctioning over the last hour during this, erm, event..."

"Very strange," muttered the head. "Very peculiar. Anyhow, I have lots to do for the rest of the day. I guess we will cast this phantasmagoria aside for a moment, and continue on our day."

And the head walked away, as did Grace rather hesitantly. "I'm always here for a chat Grace if you need one; or even if you want to discuss some William Blake..." She smiled and disappeared into the playground.

I walked back to my classroom and up the stairs, then found the cubicle I had sat in just an hour before. I thought of everything that had occurred during this bizarre episode and wondered what the rest of the community thought about it, and whether Grace was a threat, or just needed some help. I would definitely keep an eye on her in the future, if only to see if she was okay.

But out of all of this, what had become clear was that two worlds had come together to save the day. The world of the Quran, and the world of English literature. I had used Quranic verses, and the verses of Blake, to protect myself, my school, and to bring a poor, little soul back into the community. My Muslim interior and Western exterior could fuse, bond, merge and express a unique manifestation of both realities. The two worlds could live together in my mind and heart, and they could be used for the benefit of the rest of the community. I did belong here, in a very complicated and inextricable way. I looked down at the Hulk on my boxers who seemed to be smiling back at me. But suddenly there was a knock on the door. I hastily finished, washed my hands, dried them and opened the door. A random, blue classroom chair stood still outside my cubicle door, very still, and rather ominous. Suddenly I heard a scream. I yelped.

Then Trudy and Jayden stuck their heads from around the corner and laughed: "Just having you on sir!"

I lost my patience: "Oh shut up you MUPPETS!"

Novid Shaid is an English teacher and writer of novels, short stories and poetry.

Born and brought up in Aylesbury in the UK, Novid developed a love for writing stories and reading English literature as a child, which culminated in him later becoming an English teacher in local secondary schools. In 2014, Novid published his first novel, the mystical thriller, The Hidden Ones and thereafter he published a book of short stories and poetry on Amazon.

He shares short stories and poems on his website: www.novid.co.uk